ESKIMO KIDS
ALONE IN THE ARCTIC

Copyright © 2014 by Ronald E. Brechner
All rights reserved.
ISBN: 1500147893
ISBN-13: 978-1500147891
Library of Congress Control Number: 2014914444
CreateSpace Independent Publishing Platform, North Charleston, SC

Illustrated by Katrina Brechner
Edited by Diane Brechner

First Edition

CONTENTS

CHAPTER 1
Living in the Arctic

Years ago, there was an Eskimo family with two Eskimo children named Nenaw and Sitka. Nenaw was the older brother, age thirteen, and his sister Sitka was only eleven –but she was a smart eleven. They lived together in northern Alaska, inside the Arctic Circle, where temperatures get very, very cold.

Their house wasn't made of wood or brick, which can take months to build. Eskimos can build their houses, called igloos, in a couple of days. Smaller igloos may take only a few hours to build. The family cuts the hardened snow into blocks with a long knife. They stack the snow blocks together to make the walls and then angle the stacked blocks toward the center to form a dome for the roof.

Their igloo had snow walls and a snow ceiling. How would you like to live in a house made of snow?

The tunnel entrance they made helped to keep out the cold wind and the wild animals. At the very top of the igloo ceiling, the final block of snow was left out so that smoke from a small fire could escape and this would also let the air circulate. Nenaw and Sitka's igloo was special because their dad, Pano, had poked a hole in the snow wall on each side and then placed a sheet of ice over each hole. These were like windows made of ice instead of glass, which allowed the light to come in during the daytime but would keep everything else out, especially the wind and snow.

Even though the igloo was made of hard snow and ice, a small fire would keep the Eskimo family warm without melting their home. Does that seem amazing?

The igloo was only one small room, but it contained the family's belongings and kept them safe and secure.

In the middle of winter, there wasn't much wood around to collect for a fire, so the family burned animal fat, called blubber, usually coming from a whale, seal or sea lion. They also ate the blubber, which helped to keep them warm in the sub-zero Arctic temperatures.

You probably have many clothes, but Nenaw and Sitka only had one set of clothes. Each of them had a seal skin hat to keep their heads dry. In fact, their hats were decorated with animal bones, beads and drawings they made. Each of them also had a big furry coat with a hood. Nenaw's coat was made from a polar bear skin and the hood was bordered with wolf fur. The fur was so long and thick that when Nenaw covered his head with the hood, the fur protected his face from freezing in the fierce, cold wind. Pano, their father, had killed the animals with his spear to collect leather hides and furs for making warm, strong clothing. Chena, their mother, sewed their clothing together using needles made out of bone. She sometimes had to chew the leather to soften it, especially when making gloves and boots.

CHAPTER 2
Fishing and a Storm

One day their parents, Chena and Pano, went fishing. They were in the small kayak, which Pano had built. Since there was only room for two, the couple paddled out among the icebergs to fish while the children stayed ashore. The icebergs towered over the kayak, and for every part of an iceberg that was visible above water, it was nine times bigger underwater, sometimes stretching for miles.

While the adults fished, a terrible storm suddenly moved in. The wind caused huge waves to break off large chunks of ice from the shore, forming even more icebergs.

The wind and waves were too strong for Pano and Chena to paddle against. The small kayak was swept away from shore and out to sea, banging into the icebergs over and over. Pano and Chena were helplessly driven farther and farther toward the ocean until Nenaw and Sitka finally lost sight of them.

CHAPTER 3
Eskimo Kids Left Alone

The fierce storm almost froze Nenaw and Sitka right where they stood. The blowing snow, which blocked Nenaw and Sitka's vision, was piling up around them and quickly covering their tracks. After waiting for their parents for what seemed like forever, Nenaw told his sister that they must leave. "We need to try to find our way back to the family igloo," he said. Although Sitka didn't want to go away without her mom and dad, she was getting very cold and knew that her brother was right. Helping each other, they pushed against the storm and began struggling in the general direction of the igloo – always holding hands.

It's a good thing that Nenaw had a keen sense of direction or they never would have found the igloo. Once inside, Nenaw worked fast to get a small fire started. The shelter of the igloo and the warm fire kept them safe from the storm outside.

"Will Mommy and Daddy be back?" asked a worried Sitka.

"Maybe tomorrow," responded Nenaw, "For now, we should try to sleep."

To get their beds ready, each of them spread animal furs over blocks of solid ice. Both kids were exhausted from their struggle to get back to the igloo and quickly fell asleep. Could you sleep on a block of ice?

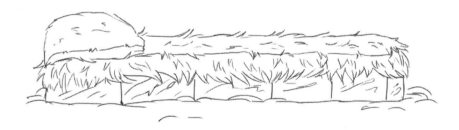

The next morning, Pano and Chena didn't come home.

"Maybe tomorrow," said Nenaw. As the blizzard continued raging outside, they didn't come; and they didn't come the next day, or the next, or the next. Pano and Chena never did return. The Eskimo kids were now orphans—they didn't have a mom or dad anymore. In fact, they were completely alone in the barren, ice-covered Arctic.

Both kids, from the time they could walk, had worked beside their parents. During those years they learned many of the Eskimo survival tricks. But was that enough? The Arctic was a dangerous place.

They had food stored in or near the igloo that the two of them could eat for a month if they were careful, but both of them knew that they would have to hunt and fish to build up their food supply for the dark months ahead. Sooner or later, they would need to repair their clothes and even make new clothing as they grew. Collecting blubber and oil would also be necessary for food, fire, and light. These were big jobs for grown-ups and seemed almost impossible for a thirteen and eleven year old.

Nenaw assured Sitka that he would protect her and see that they always had food and fire. He was so confident and brave that she believed him and trusted him.

"He won't let anything happen to me," she whispered under her breath.

CHAPTER 4
Seal Hunting

It had been a week since the blizzard had passed. The Eskimo kids were still alone and the reality now settled into their minds that their parents were not coming home.

Nenaw got up early in the morning on the eighth day and rubbed blubber all over his body. The oil would act as a protective coating for his skin and help him to keep warm. He put on seal skin pants followed by a pair of caribou skin pants. He then put on fur stockings and waterproof moccasins made of seal skin. Over these he laced his caribou skin boots. Feet ready!

Next came his big polar bear skin coat with the wolf fur hood. Pulling his seal skin cap tightly over his head, he then picked up his dad's rifle, loaded it, and slipped some extra bullets into the deep pocket of his jacket. It was O.K. because Pano had taught him how to shoot and how to take care of the rifle.

In the freezing Arctic, when the bright sunlight glares off of the surface of the snow it can temporarily blind you. This is called snow blindness. Nenaw took glasses made of caribou bone with narrow slits carved out for eyeholes and slipped them into his pocket. The bone would block the bright light reflected off the snow while the slits would allow him to see clearly.

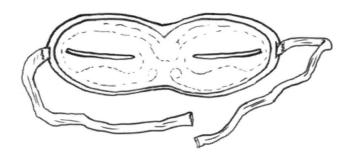

After putting on his mittens, he crawled out of the tunnel into the bright daylight. It was that time of year in the Arctic Circle, when the days were longer than the nights. During the other half of the year, darkness would rule as daylight became less and less. Nenaw had to become a great hunter, fast – while the days were still bright and long.

Sitka stayed at the igloo doing her chores. After mending a worn stocking, she prepared for nightfall by filling a lamp with seal oil, then went out to the ice hole used for a freezer and removed a stringer of fish to feed to the sled dogs. This she did by standing back from the dogs and throwing the fish to them. She was very careful not to get too close to the dogs when they were hungry.

Meanwhile, Nenaw walked about two miles before he spotted seals lying around a hole in the ice. As he approached them, they quickly waddled over and plunged back through the hole. GONE! How would he be able to shoot any if they disappeared into the water so quickly?

Remembering a survival trick that his dad had taught him, Nenaw scraped together loose snow into a waist-high pile. Walking over to the edge of the hole, he used his gun handle to scratch and tap on the ice. Then he rushed back to the pile of snow and lay next to it on the ground. He used his arms and gun handle to pull the loose snow on top of himself to cover most of his body. The seals wouldn't notice his eyes peering out of the snow, or his gun, which he held in his hand, ready to shoot.

A few minutes later, the curious seals began popping their heads out of the water looking for the source of the mysterious scratching and tapping noises. Seeing nothing except a pile of snow, the seals began climbing out. All seven seals came out of the hole and once again relaxed on the ice. Slowly, Nenaw moved his arm and aimed the gun. Blam, Blam, Blam, Blam, Blam!! Four seals escaped, but Nenaw had shot three of the seven. That was pretty good shooting for his first time hunting by himself. He would now have food, skins, meat for the dogs, bones, and oil for the lamp.

The seals were too heavy for Nenaw to carry, so he headed back home to get the dogsled. It was a good thing that it stayed light outside for a long time. Upon arriving back at the igloo, he crawled in through the tunnel and excitedly told Sitka about his success. She was now needed to help bring the seals home. Sitka dressed warmly while Nenaw hooked the dogs one-by-one to the dogsled. She came out carrying two large furs and climbed into the dogsled. The furs would cover her to keep her warm. Nenaw handed her the gun to carry, along with one of his spears. Everything was set.

"Mush," yelled Nenaw. The dogs, needing a good run, lurched ahead. Nenaw stood on the runners at the back of the dogsled and hung onto the handles at the top of the sled. Five of the dogs were used to pull the sled, while two dogs were left behind to protect the igloo.

CHAPTER 5
The Wolves and the Walrus

Wow! They covered the two miles back to the seals in great time. The dogs were fast and powerful. As the water hole came into view, the kids were surprised to see a pack of five wolves in the distance, also heading toward the seals. Nenaw urged the dogs to go faster, needing to beat the wolves to the ice hole. The dogsled arrived first. Nenaw grabbed the rifle and shot into the air to try to frighten the wolves away. Sitka brought him the spear – shaking it while yelling loudly. The wolves were startled by the noise, but didn't leave. They made a large circle around the kids and began to attack from all directions.

Each wolf watched for an opportunity to leap into the center, trying to bite someone or something. One even got close enough to bite the thumb off of Sitka's mitten.

But don't worry – these Eskimos made mittens that have an extra thumb-warming hole inside. When the thumb cover of the mitten gets cold, they move their thumb inside a pocket beside their fingers to keep it warm.

The wolf had bitten off the empty thumb of her mitten, so Sitka was not hurt.

The wolves tightened their circle, moving closer and closer. Finally, Nenaw managed to shoot one of the wolves. It stumbled and fell next to the dogsled and the dogs immediately pounced on the wolf and ate it for supper. The rest of the wolves renewed their attack and were closing in on their prey when a large walrus burst through the ice hole. It used its long tusks to stick into the ice and pull itself out of the water. Walruses can be as big as a car and can weigh as much as 3,000 pounds. It started toward the wolves, who quickly went on the attack. One wolf attempted to rip a piece of meat off the walrus, but the wolf was quickly pierced by the walrus' tusk. Walrus tusks can grow to be three feet long, and as the wolves soon learned, the tusks can be deadly. The walrus then grabbed the wolf with its mouth and flipped it high into the air. When the wolf hit the ground, it was dead.

While the walrus and wolves were busy fighting each other, the Eskimo kids quietly dragged the seals over to the dogsled and loaded them. Sitka climbed on with the seals. The surviving wolves retreated. Even though the walrus was injured, it was still fighting mad as it turned toward the kids.

"Mush," yelled Nenaw, and the dogsled sped away.

They had barely escaped with their lives. On the way back to the igloo, Nenaw kept thinking about that huge walrus. Its blubber would make oil for fires and the meat could supply them with food for several months. That did it! He decided to drop off Sitka and the seals and head straight back to the water hole to finish off the walrus.

CHAPTER 6
Nenaw Is Trapped

Sitka helped unload the seals. Nenaw grabbed a second spear, reloaded the rifle and headed back to the water hole. As he approached the hole in the ice, he counted three dead wolves. The large walrus was still there, but was bleeding and not moving. Maybe it was dead. This was a surprise! Nenaw grabbed his spear and walked toward the walrus. Suddenly, the walrus reared up and charged toward Nenaw, who barely had time to react.

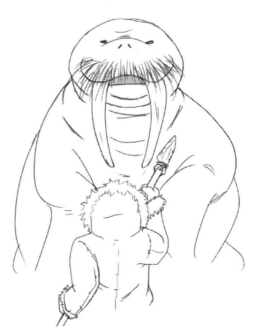

As the walrus lunged, Nenaw lifted the sharpened end of the spear up toward the walrus and braced the blunt end against the ice. The walrus came down on the spear, plunging the spearhead deep into its body. That finished it! As the walrus' body fell to the ground, part of it fell on Nenaw, pinning his legs. No matter how hard he pulled, he couldn't get his legs out from under the weight of the walrus.

"Here, boy!" yelled Nenaw, "Come here, boy." Slowly the sled dogs came over to him, dragging the sled behind them. Nenaw was able to get a good grip on the sled, and while holding on tightly with both hands, he yelled, "Mush!" The dogs leaped forward, but it didn't work. After several more tries, the dogs were still unable to pull him free so he called for them to stop. Nenaw then had another idea. He took out his long knife and chipped away at the ice under his legs, relieving some of the pressure caused by the heavy walrus.

Again, Nenaw grabbed the dogsled and hung on tightly. "Mush!" he yelled. The dogs again sprang forward, and this time they gradually pulled him free. Good, his legs were fine. How in the world could so much happen in one day? He now had several wolf furs plus one big walrus and plenty of meat for the dogs. There was a lot of work ahead of him, but he smiled – like the great hunter he was!

The wolves were hauled home in one trip, but the walrus took Nenaw several trips because he had to cut it into many smaller pieces. Back at the igloo, Sitka and Nenaw got ready to skin, chunk, and clean the animals. The large walrus tusks would make good knife handles and many other accessories. The kids could even use the stringy muscle tissue of the wolves to make a strong string for sewing. Some of the hide would be made into strong leather twine for lacing boots and for tying down almost anything.

It took four days for the brother and sister to skin and prepare the various animal parts. Each night they fell into the fur on their ice block beds and even though it was still light outside they slept like babies. They now had most of the supplies that they would need to survive several more months in the Arctic.

CHAPTER 7
Chasing Caribou

As the days shortened and the nights became longer, Nenaw grew tired of eating seal meat, wolf meat, and blubber. Caribou tracks were a common sight and he occasionally saw caribou moving across the distant horizon. One morning, Nenaw woke up to find several feet of fresh new snow. He and Sitka put on snowshoes, which looked a bit like tennis rackets strapped to the bottoms of their boots.

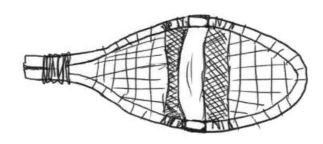

When they went outside these funny-looking shoe bottoms kept them from sinking into the snow. Sitka with a spear and Nenaw with his gun and a spear, started out to hunt caribou. In a short time, they saw one in the distance struggling to run, but because it was so heavy it kept sinking up to its chest in the soft, deep snow.

The snowshoes kept the Eskimos on top of the snow and made it easy for them to catch up to the caribou. It was easy pickin's. The Eskimo kids would now have the hide they needed for pants, boots and other clothing – along with tasty meat for cooking. Yum!!

CHAPTER 8
Victory Ride

Nenaw and Sitka knew that their parents rarely had visitors. Maybe one visitor every two years would come by. There were people out there somewhere – but where? Sometimes the kids would hook up the dogsled and go exploring. Nenaw would drive, while Sitka rode in the dogsled. They never saw signs of other people. But it was on one of these exploring expeditions that they came across a polar bear. In fact, they came around a big ice pile and nearly ran smack dab into it.

The bear rose up on its hind legs, growling fiercely. It must have been seven feet tall. The dogs swerved to avoid the bear, but the sled almost hit it. With a wide swipe of its paw, the bear ripped the back of the dogsled completely off and sent Nenaw flying through the air. He landed tumbling and rolling.

Nenaw's gun and spear were still in the broken front half of the sled, which had been pulled several yards away before Sitka was able to stop the dogs. The snarling polar bear slowly advanced toward Nenaw, who was defenseless, having no gun or spear—only his knife. He thought he would surely die and be eaten because bears are too fast to outrun.

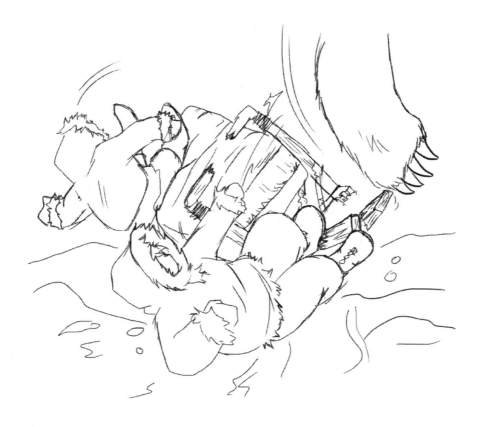

Sitka grabbed the spear from the dogsled – but then had a better idea. She went around to the front of the sled and quickly began letting the dogs loose. As each dog was released, it charged after the bear. Soon, the polar bear was busy slashing and fighting with all of the dogs. The dogs attacked from all sides, giving Nenaw the opportunity to grab Sitka's spear and join the fight. He jabbed with the spear and then jumped back.

Nenaw kept fighting, jumping in and out of the battle, each time poking the bear with his spear.   One-by-one, the dogs bit at the bear, but as the bear hit them with its clawed paws, they received deep cuts and gashes and some were flung through the air. It was a losing battle. The bear was winning!

Finally, Nenaw desperately threw his spear at the bear's chest and ran toward the dogsled. Sitka quickly held out the loaded gun and Nenaw grabbed it. As he swung around, the polar bear crashed into him.

The crash caused the gun to fire and both Nenaw and the bear fell across the already broken dogsled, further destroying it. The bear started to get up. Sitka began clubbing it in the head with a piece of broken dogsled. The bear raised up its head and opened its jaws to attack Sitka, but instead fell over dead. Sitka helped Nenaw stand and they held each other tightly. *They had just killed a polar bear!*

When the kids examined the bear closely, they found the head of Nenaw's spear buried in its chest. More importantly, the bear's collision with the gun had caused it to fire the fatal shot, which meant the bear had actually shot itself.

Yes, the bear was dead, but how were they going to get it back to the igloo? They couldn't waste it, because they would need the fur and the meat. The kids were both exhausted, the dogsled was a wreck, and it was too late in the day to figure out what to do next.

"We'll just build a small igloo to sleep in safely for the night, and then head home tomorrow," said Nenaw. Sitka agreed and they began cutting blocks of packed snow. Within a couple of hours they had built a very small igloo for protection. Z-Z-Z-Z-Z

It was light outside when they woke up the next morning. Out on the ice, they were happy to find that several of their sled dogs had not run away. Although the sled was ruined, all of the harnesses were still good. Nenaw began harnessing the dogs, and then together he and Sitka hooked the harnessed dogs to the bear's feet. Sitka climbed up onto the polar bear's belly and Nenaw handed her their supplies. He then went up front with the dogs and put one of the empty harnesses around himself.

"Mush," said Sitka. The dogs (and Nenaw) began pulling. Once they got the bear moving, it glided smoothly across the ice. Nenaw and the dogs pulled the bear with Sitka riding on top all the way back to their igloo.

THE END

BE SURE TO WATCH FOR MORE ADVENTURES WITH THE
ESKIMO KIDS!

Made in the USA
Lexington, KY
30 January 2015